My Little Brother Ben

by Karen Cogan

illustrated by Meryl Treatner

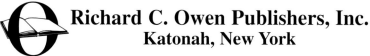

Richard C. Owen Publishers, Inc.
Katonah, New York

I built a tower.

Ben knocked it down.

He cried.

I built a bridge.

Ben knocked it down.

He cried.

I opened a book.

Ben sat beside me.

I read him a story.

The Green Mountain Road

Ben smiled.